World Series SUPERSTARS

Josh Beckett
and the FLORIDA MARLINS

2003 WORLD SERIES

by Michael Sandler

Consultant: Jim Sherman
Head Baseball Coach
University of Delaware

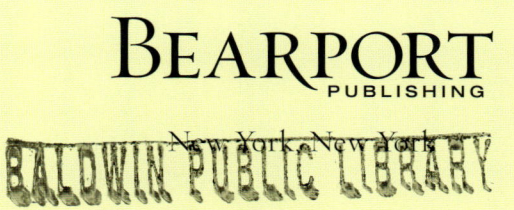

BEARPORT
PUBLISHING

New York, New York

Credits
Cover and Title Page, © Ezra Shaw/Getty Images; 4, © REUTERS/Ray Stubblebine; 5, © REUTERS/Mike Blake; 6, © Courtesy of Lynn Beckett; 7, © Darren Carroll Photography; 9, © Ronald C. Modra/Sports Imagery/Getty Images; 10, © AP Images/Don Frazier; 11, Rhona Wise/AFP/Getty Images; 12, © AP Images/Wilfredo Lee; 13, © Pierre DuCharme/Reuters/Corbis; 14, © Matthew Stockman/Getty Images; 15, © REUTERS/Marc Serota; 16, © Denis Bancroft/Florida Marlins/MLB Photos via Getty Images; 17, © Mike Segar/Reuters/Corbis; 18, © Jed Jacobsohn/Getty Images; 19, © REUTERS/Mike Blake; 20, © G. Paul Burnett/The New York Times/Redux; 21, © Jamie Squire/Getty Images; 22T, © AP Photo/Ben Margot; 22C, © Ezra Shaw/Getty Images; 22B, © Robert Seale/TSN/Icon SMI.

Publisher: Kenn Goin
Senior Editor: Lisa Wiseman
Creative Director: Spencer Brinker
Photo Researcher: Omni-Photo Communications, Inc.
Design: Stacey May

Library of Congress Cataloging-in-Publication Data

Sandler, Michael.
 Josh Beckett and the Florida Marlins : 2003 World Series / by Michael Sandler ; consultant, Jim Sherman.
   p. cm. — (World Series superstars)
 Includes bibliographical references and index.
 ISBN-13: 978-1-59716-639-3 (library binding)
 ISBN-10: 1-59716-639-1 (library binding)
 1. Beckett, Josh. 2. Pitchers (Baseball)—Florida—Biography. 3. Baseball players—Florida—Biography. 4. Florida Marlins (Baseball team) I. Title.

GV865.B43S36 2008
796.357092—dc22
 (B)
                    2007033121

Copyright © 2008 Bearport Publishing Company, Inc. All rights reserved. No part of this publication may be reproduced in whole or in part, stored in a retrieval system, or transmitted in any form or by any means, electronic, mechanical, photocopying, recording, or otherwise, without written permission from the publisher.

For more information, write to Bearport Publishing Company, Inc., 101 Fifth Avenue, Suite 6R, New York, New York 10003. Printed in the United States of America.

10 9 8 7 6 5 4 3 2 1

Contents

A Big Night 4

Kid Heat 6

Top Pick 8

Rising Star 10

Turnaround Team 12

Playoff Surprise 14

The World Series 16

Battling Back 18

Time to Shine 20

Key Players 22

Glossary 23

Bibliography 24

Read More 24

Learn More Online 24

Index 24

A Big Night

It was a big night for Florida. The Marlins had a chance to win the 2003 World Series. To do it, they needed to stop the New York Yankees.

The Marlins' manager, Jack McKeon, picked 23-year-old Josh Beckett to start Game 6. People thought Jack was crazy. How could young Josh pitch with only three days rest? Why not use another pitcher?

Jack didn't care. His mind was made up. Rested or not, he wanted Josh on the **mound**.

Marlins manager Jack McKeon

Josh Beckett on the mound at the start of Game 6

Starting pitchers usually get four or five days rest between games. Josh had never pitched with only three days off.

Kid Heat

Josh was from Spring, Texas, a small town near Houston. Growing up, he liked outdoor sports such as hunting and fishing.

However, baseball was his first love. He began playing at age five. Even in Little League, he threw the ball hard. It flew through the air as fast as a rocket.

Josh began high school with an 85-mile-per-hour (137-k-p-h) **fastball**. It got faster and faster each year until it hit 97 miles per hour (156 kph). Batters couldn't handle his pitches.

Josh in his Little League uniform

Josh was named *USA Today*'s High School Pitcher of the Year in 1999.

Playing for Spring High School, Josh got the nickname "Kid Heat." *Heat* is a baseball term for super-fast pitching.

Top Pick

In the late 1990s, Josh became the country's top high-school pitcher. **Scouts** from **major league** teams flew in to watch him. Their eyes popped at his speeding fastball. They shook their heads at his impossible-to-hit **curveball**.

Scouts weren't just wowed by Josh's arm. His brain was just as sharp. He seemed to know everything about pitching.

When the 1999 **draft** came around, it was no surprise that Josh was the first pitcher chosen. The Florida Marlins were the lucky team.

Josh's rookie baseball card

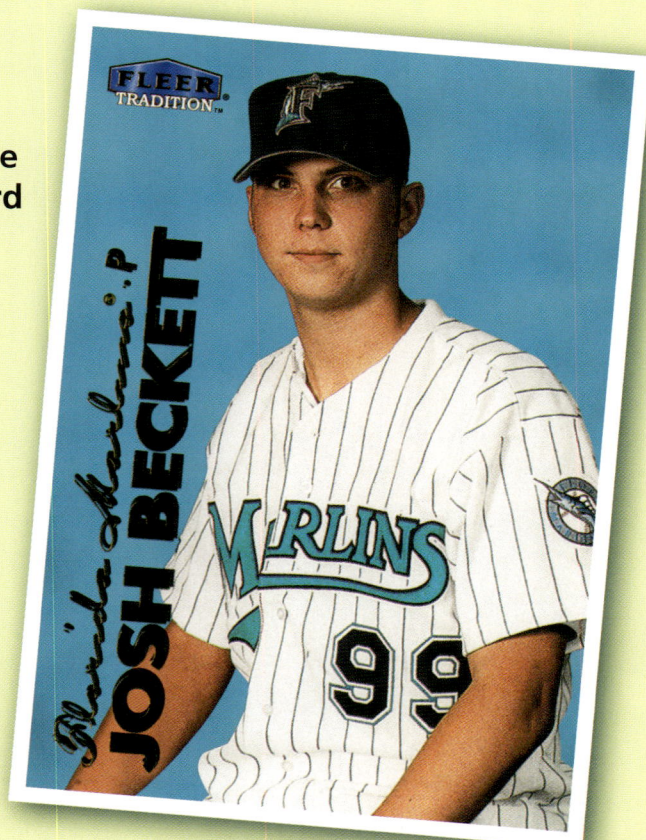

Josh reminded scouts of another Texas pitcher—baseball's all-time **strikeout** king, Nolan Ryan.

Nolan Ryan is the only pitcher to strike out 5,000 batters.

Rising Star

Josh moved quickly through Florida's **minor-league** teams. Along the way, he piled up wins and strikeouts. Clearly, he was ready for the **big leagues**.

In September 2001, he joined Florida's major-league team. The Marlins knew Josh would be a star. The only question was how long it would take.

Unfortunately for Josh, injuries hurt him his first two seasons. He spent as much time on the **disabled list** as he did pitching.

Josh during spring training in 2000

Josh won his first major-league game, 8-1.

Josh pitched fewer than 200 innings in the minor leagues. Even so, he was named 2001 Minor League Player of the Year.

Turnaround Team

As Josh struggled with injuries, Florida struggled to win games. The team played poorly in 2002.

Early in the 2003 season, things grew really bad. The Marlins had baseball's worst record. Hoping to change things, the team fired its manager.

The new manager, Jack McKeon, turned the team around. Pitchers started throwing strikes. Batters began hitting. Florida started winning.

The Marlins snuck into the **playoffs**. In the first round, they beat the San Francisco Giants.

Jack McKeon (#15) talks to his players on the field.

Jack told his players to "have fun" on the field. Pitcher Dontrelle Willis did, winning nine times and only losing once.

Jack McKeon had over 700 wins as a manager. However, he had never won a World Series.

Playoff Surprise

Next up were the Chicago Cubs. Led by big-hitting Sammy Sosa, the Cubs were a powerful team. When Chicago won three of the first four games, Florida's season seemed close to an end.

Then Josh stepped in for Game 5. He pitched an incredible **complete game**, which Florida won, 4-0.

The Marlins went on to win Game 6, too. The series was now tied. The teams would have to play a **winner-take-all** seventh game.

Josh held Sammy Sosa hitless in Game 5.

The first team to get four wins would move on to the World Series.

The Game 5 victory was Josh's first complete game since high school.

The World Series

In Game 7, Josh came through again. Pitching in **relief**, he **retired** 12 out of 13 batters. Florida beat Chicago, moving on to the World Series.

The Marlins' **opponents** were the New York Yankees. Unlike Florida, the Yankees made it to the World Series almost every year. Most of the time they won!

Florida surprised the Yankees by taking the opening game. New York came back to win Game 2.

Marlins catcher Ivan Rodriguez (middle) is congratulated by a teammate after he scored during Game 7 against the Cubs.

Hideki Matsui hit a three-run home run to help the Yankees win Game 2.

The New York Yankees had played in six of the eight World Series from 1996 to 2003.

Battling Back

In Game 3, Josh got his chance to pitch. His pitches were perfect. The first ten Yankees batters couldn't get a hit.

Then New York showed why they had won so many **titles**. Twice, Yankees **shortstop** Derek Jeter doubled and came home to score. Florida lost the game.

Still, the Marlins came back to win Games 4 and 5. They had three of the four wins they needed. One more and the Marlins would be the champions.

Derek Jeter at bat in Game 3

Florida had won a World Series only once before, in 1997.

Shortstop Alex Gonzalez's home run won Game 4 for the Marlins.

Time to Shine

Florida's manager believed Josh could get them the win they needed. He made Josh the starter of Game 6 even though he had only three days of rest.

When the game began, Josh proved his manager right. Time and again, he struck out the Yankees' batters.

Florida scored in the fifth inning and then again in the sixth. The two runs were all the Marlins needed. Josh held New York scoreless until the end of the game.

The young star had shined the brightest. Josh and the Marlins were champions!

Josh (right) tags out the Yankees' Jorge Posada to end Game 6.

Josh was named Most Valuable Player (MVP) of the series.

Key Players

Josh, along with some other key players, helped the Florida Marlins win the 2003 World Series.

Josh Beckett #21
Starting Pitcher
- Bats: Right
- Throws: Right
- Born: 5/15/1980 in Spring, Texas
- Height: 6'5" (1.96 m)
- Weight: 190 pounds (86 kg)

Series Highlight
In Game 6, held the Yankees to five hits in a complete-game shutout

Brad Penny #31
Starting Pitcher
- Bats: Right
- Throws: Right
- Born: 5/24/1978 in Blackwell, Oklahoma
- Height: 6'4" (1.93 m)
- Weight: 200 pounds (91 kg)

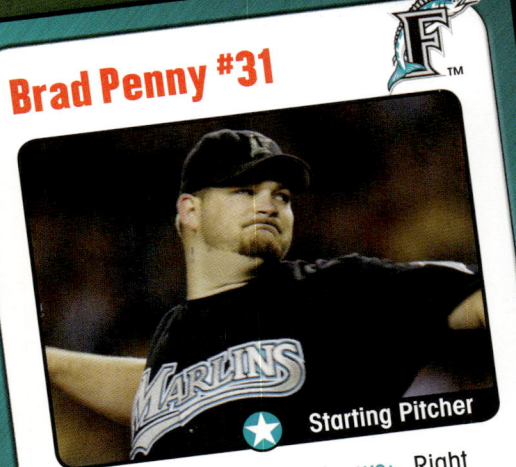

Series Highlights
Won two games as the starting pitcher

Alex Gonzalez #11
Shortstop
- Bats: Right
- Throws: Right
- Born: 2/15/1977 in Cagua, Venezuela
- Height: 6'0" (1.83 m)
- Weight: 170 pounds (77 kg)

Series Highlights
Homered to win Game 4; scored winning run in Game 6

Glossary

big leagues (BIG LEEGZ) the major leagues

complete game (kuhm-PLEET GAME) when a starting pitcher pitches for the entire game

curveball (KURV-bawl) a pitch thrown so that it curves as it gets closer to the batter

disabled list (diss-AY-buhld LIST) a list of players who are hurt and cannot play in games

draft (DRAFT) an event in which young players are chosen by major-league teams

fastball (FAST-bawl) a pitch thrown as hard and quick as possible

major league (MAY-jur LEEG) the highest level of professional baseball in the United States, made up of the American League and the National League

minor league (MYE-nur LEEG) baseball teams run by major-league teams that train young players

mound (MOUND) a small hill on the baseball field where a pitcher stands to throw the ball

opponents (uh-POH-nuhnts) teams or athletes who others play against in a sporting event

playoffs (PLAY-awfss) games held after the regular season to determine who will play in the World Series

relief (ri-LEEF) when a pitcher comes into a game, after it has begun, to replace another pitcher

retired (ri-TYE-urd) when a pitcher gets a batter out

scouts (SKOUTS) people who search for talented young players for major-league teams

shortstop (SHORT-stop) the player whose position is between second and third base

starting pitchers (START-ing PICH-urz) pitchers who play at the beginning of games

strikeout (STRIKE-out) when a batter swings at and misses three pitches or when the umpire calls the batter out after the third strike is thrown

titles (TYE-tuhlz) championships; in baseball, World Series wins

winner-take-all (WIN-ur-TAYKE-AWL) a single game that decides which team will win a title

23

Bibliography

Schlossberg, Dan, with Kevin Baxter. *Miracle Over Miami: How the 2003 Marlins Shocked the World.* Champaign, IL: Sports Publishing (2004).

The Dallas Morning News

Sports Illustrated

Read More

DK Publishing. *World Series (Eyewitness Books).* New York: DK (2004).

Peterson, Sheryl. *The Story of the Florida Marlins.* Mankato, MN: Creative Education (2007).

Teitelbaum, Michael. *National League East.* Mankato, MN: Child's World (2007).

Learn More Online

To learn more about Josh Beckett, the Florida Marlins, and the World Series, visit
www.bearportpublishing.com/WorldSeriesSuperstars

Index

Chicago Cubs 14, 16
curveball 8
draft 8
fastball 6–7, 8
Gonzalez, Alex 19, 22
injuries 10, 12
Jeter, Derek 18
major leagues 8, 10–11
McKeon, Jack 4, 12–13, 20
minor leagues 10–11
MVP 21
New York Yankees 4, 16–17, 18, 20
Penny, Brad 22
playoffs 12, 14–15, 16
Ryan, Nolan 9
San Francisco Giants 12
Sosa, Sammy 14
Spring, Texas 6–7

NO LONGER THE PROPERTY OF BALDWIN PUBLIC LIBRARY

3 1115 00560 7683

```
J 796.357 S           22.61
Sandler, Michael
Josh beckett and the
florida marlins.
2003 world series.
```

6/25   7× 8/15/2012

BALDWIN PUBLIC LIBRARY

2385 GRAND AVENUE

BALDWIN, N.Y. 11510-3289

(516) 223-6228

DEMCO